The Background Book Serie: ## The Rulebook Serie:

Please search by book Title
Please search by book Title

Please search by book Title

Si vous préférez lire en français, jetez un œil ici :

Sera disponible bientôt.

Si prefieres leer en español, échale un vistazo aquí:

Falls du lieber in Deutsch liest, schaue doch am besten hier:

Fantasy Battles: The Ninth Age:
Ask the Sage

Impressum:

Written by the T9A Team

Published by FlorianGressConsulting, Rosenweg 24, 93053 Regensburg, Germany

Printed by Amazon Media EU S.à r.l., 5 Rue Plaetis, L-2338, Luxembourg

ISBN: 978-3-98807-009-8

THE IX AGE
FANTASY BATTLES

ASK THE SAGE

Frequently Asked Questions About the Ninth Age

THE IX AGE
FANTASY BATTLES

ASK THE SAGE

Education is a fine thing, and the citizens of Avras are naturally curious. Many are the questions they have about the strange peoples and places we find today in the Ninth Age. To shine a light on such matters, we naturally turned to the legendary Sigmund "The Sage" Selig, that most good natured and fair-minded of scholars, who can be found in his rather cramped offices above the Unnatural Philosophy department on Via Urbana.

Written and edited by the Background Team

Head of Background
Edward Murdoch

Art Direction
Casp

Layout
Neil Foster

Art Prompts
Casp, Karanadon,
Erik Aronson

February 2024

BEAST HERDS

What kind of society and hierarchies exist among the herds, and how do their largest monsters fit within this structure?

A fascinating subject – you'll have to read my papers on the matter, but I suppose I can provide a short summary. Beasts naturally form bachelor herds, much like non-intelligent migratory bovidae, with the division between Hidden Herds and War Herds forming the foundation of their society. Unlike common cattle, however, this society exhibits many further complexities. Hierarchies are formed by both popular acclaim and leadership challenge, though not at the same time; popularity is rarely challenged, being achieved by recognition for one's cleverness and cunning, or by having the best tales – told either by oneself or about oneself.

Field reports suggest that common beasts and minotaurs form the bulk of herd society and leadership. The stranger and larger creatures produced by more adventurous womb-marking stand somewhat outside of such hierarchies. They mostly live with the Hidden Herds and are treated as brothers or children, but lack the desire or perhaps the mental capacity to seek power for themselves.

What is the herds' relationship with other species and nations? What motivates them to attack us? In what light do they view the sylvan elves, with whom they share the forests?

You must understand, the herds are at home in the wild, seeing themselves as the agents of nature itself. To them, advanced sedentary cultures are not civilised but unnatural. Meanwhile, humans, elves and dwarves view beasts as the ultimate outsiders, symbolising the very dangers of the primitive wilderness.

The herds' violent reputation is largely the result of regular and unprovoked attacks on sedentary peoples. The reasons are numerous – plunder of resources, slave-taking, mercenary employment and often simply prestige, since war is a good way to forge one's story. The reports I trust suggest that they don't actually enjoy violence for its own sake, but are not shy about harming those who fail to respect natural law if they gain something valuable. In such respects, they differ little from human barbarians.

A final motivation, of course, is vengeance for attacks against themselves. The imbeciles in military command have rarely understood this point when I've explained it to them. Even when I speak extra loudly and slowly.

It's unclear how the herds feel about the sylvan fae – I'd guess that they likely see little difference between human and elf. It's not precisely true to say they "share" the forests – herds do live in such areas, but they are just as often found in other terrain, and they see all of nature as their domain.

Do beasts make use of captured technology? And what prevents them from building war machines, if even the Warborn can manage it?

Beasts are indeed known to make use of stolen items, as long as they are portable. They especially prize arcane treasures and spellbooks. Complex technologies such as firearms are less valuable, since they can't be maintained in working condition for long.

It's true that the herds have shown little interest in constructing machines. I'm inclined to agree with Pernovich's assessment that they innately distrust complex mechanisms as antithetical to nature. But an equally likely explanation is the pragmatic one – inventing and building advanced devices is very challenging when one must constantly move to find food. Even the Warborn have sedentary settlements, where goblins are known to tinker. The herds do not.

Is there a language of mutual intelligibility between the herds and other species, such that they could communicate if need arises?

Beasts lack the necessary vocal cords for language as we know it, but this limitation has been overcome in rare cases by specialised womb-markings. Herd Speakers have played an important role in what little diplomacy has been achieved historically by the herds. And many beasts have a good ear for languages and music, often being able to understand even where they cannot speak.

Equally, I've heard tell of certain elves and humans who have learned to mimic the herds' own languages – at least to an extent. The grunting and gesturing is one thing, but the musk scents are quite another. Of course, beasts can in rare cases learn written language, facilitating non-verbal communication. There are even stories of kidnapping educated individuals to serve as writing tutors and scribes to record the deeds of bestial warlords. I don't envy that assignment.

I've heard of herds worshipping statues of heroes. Can they create statues of their own? Do they have artists and art forms in their own society?

Yes, beasts are known to create their own statues and totems, generally made of wood or other portable materials. The herds often leave memorials behind them, particularly around ancient trees and places of natural awe. They rarely produce their own stonework, likely owing to the demands of their nomadic lives, though they value it highly as a more lasting form of remembrance.

DAEMON LEGIONS

What goals would draw the Daemon Legions to choose to cross the Veil?

The minions of the Dark Gods seek always to tear down ordered living. Sadly, I can give all too many examples – and yet, daemons need no special reason or excuse to enter our Realm. They are always seeking to come here, where they can form tangible bodies, exert somewhat more freedom, and generally cause mayhem. Their specific motives are chaotic and varied to say the least, difficult even for such a learned man as I to ascertain.

Many daemons are opportunistic, seizing sudden chances to strike at exposed individuals or unprotected cities. Others may plot and scheme for decades, carefully manipulating many separate players in an attempt to wreak disorder on a grand scale. In most cases, they must work hand in hand with mortal cults and worshippers, who can facilitate their crossing of the Veil. But in areas of high magic they might be able to cross of their own accord, which is why real estate is so affordable around the Wasteland.

Are legions representing multiple gods more or less common than those under a single god? How are cross-pantheon forces initially formed?

The howling hordes of Hell are not renowned for their organisational skills. Opportunities for entire daemonic armies to enter the world are rare, and when they arise, all seven Dark Gods are usually interested in seizing them. For this reason, most large forces are formed of a seething mass of daemons of all kinds and affiliations, with no attempt made to divide them into different categories.

Sometimes, a single god will have a unique objective or desire and will succeed in sending a force comprised purely of its own minions. Normally, this is an attempt to prove its own greatness and glory, and very often it involves competition or outright conflict with other members of the Seven.

Where do Harbingers of Father Chaos sit within the daemonic hierarchy? Are any as powerful as a Greater Daemon?

Thorny matters of Dark Lore are the province of grim sorcerers and vile occultists – in other words, amateurs. And I am anything but that (especially if the Inquisition is asking). All I can say is that the legendary Harbingers are supposedly daemons of special constitution, seeking to represent the greatest and most mythic of entities rather than more tangible gods.

Some claim that Father Chaos is only a story or a metaphor – who can tell the truth of such deep and fundamental questions? All I can say is that Father Chaos does not act directly on this Realm, and His lack of interest apparently extends to His daemonic bannermen, who have never enjoyed the same favours as the champions of the gods. So the answer is no – I have not heard of Harbingers as powerful as the Greater Daemons.

How much do the Dark Gods care about specific regions or societies in the Mortal Realm?

The lords and denizens of the Legions usually have little interest in what they perceive as trivial details about the lands and peoples of the world, with one vital exception. They care deeply about how civilised a society is. The more that a certain culture exhibits rigid political structures, social hierarchies, punitive moral codes and any other strictures that prevent people from following their base instincts, the more that culture will incur the wrath of the Dark Gods.

It's also possible for some daemons to hold grudges or retain memories of past encounters in the Mortal Realm that may cause them to develop a fascination or hatred for a certain group or person. But these are mostly isolated cases. It's said the Wrathful Foloy's attacks on the people of Tsanas were driven by a hatred of the genial ogres' open campfires and willingness to embrace former enemies as new friends. Meanwhile, the beauty and ascetism of elves has more than once drawn the ire of those loyal to Akaan; those who refuse the Lamprey are like to find themselves devoured by it.

DREAD ELVES

Where are the oversea colonies of the Republic of Dathen? How do they differ from the mainland?

While Vetia's age of exploration is still very much in its early days, the Daeb have been plying the Nine Seas for as long as records exist. Even I don't know exactly where it keeps permanent holdings. We are aware of colonies in Virentia, known for their wine. I suspect there are also Daeb territories in Taphria and Augea – certainly there are ports and staging grounds that facilitate the activities of their global fleet.

Dathen's colonies are much like the colonies of any kingdom – ruled by expatriates from the mainland, with a culture that reflects the regional milieu, and the mercantile purpose of local operations. Even a people as wilful as the Daeb cannot prevent creolisation altogether.

Can outsiders recognise the different flavors of elf? Is it possible to immediately distinguish between Dread and Highborn?

Contrary to the ravings of Admiral Demetrieas, all elves are biologically the same species, and there is no essential or inherent element that makes an elf Daeb, Arandai or Trewi at birth. Unlike humans, physiological variations, including skin tone, do not appear to correlate to nationality – all three primary elven powers display a similar diversity. The division is purely political and cultural – elves can and have switched from one group to another.

Of course, in the majority of practical encounters, the difference is plain as day. Clothing, hair, body language, tone of voice – millennia of divergent cultural development have left the Highborn and the Dread Elves as similar as Arcalea and Åskland.

What do the Daeb typically eat?

I suspect the answer varies according to time and place. At sea, Daeb eat whatever they plunder from their raids, as well as the fish and larger creatures they take from the water – they are known to hunt the monsters of the deep for their meat, fat and oils.

In Dathen itself, they eat what they grow (or at least what their slaves grow) on the great farmlands along the Tietha river – grain, vegetables, meat and more. Thunderbeast jerky is said to be a beloved snack, commonly found on captured Daeb soldiers. I tried it once – very tough.

Do Daeb (or elves in general) have a hyper sensitive sense of smell? Are they disgusted more than humans by 'bad' smells?

There appears to be some truth to that miserable cur Minoza's claim that elven physiology is adapted to their woodland origins. Their senses are indeed more responsive than most humans'. Their ears are said to be best of all, rather than their noses.

Elves affect to be disgusted by almost everything about humanity, so it's hard to tell if their frequent insults about our odours reflect a physiological aversion or a cultural one.

Is there a significant aesthetic difference between Dread and Highborn elves, in regards to architecture, fashion, battle gear and so on?

A common question among those who – like the majority of humans – have never met either kind of elf. It only takes one encounter to learn the answer – they are aesthetically very distinct.

A full exploration of elven fashion could fill many books – too many books, in Minoza's case. Naturally, there is plenty of variation within both factions – as many subcultures and regional offshoots as any human power. In general, one can summarise by saying that the Arandai seek sophistication and the aristocrat's effortless refinement, while the Daeb seek to reflect what they call their superior self-mastery and their will to dominate.

Highborn structures are tall and serene, their clothes and armours elegant and mesmerising. Dread elf architecture is forbidding and monumental, their garments practical, austere and uncompromising.

DWARVEN HOLDS

Herr Sage, we know you know many things, but do you know the mysteries of the Seeker cult? Tell us of its gods and rituals, and its place among the Holds.

Such matters are obscure even to those who call themselves scholars, but they are no mystery to the greatest sage of the Ninth Age. I shall grant your petition and tell you of the Seekers. The cult represents the only remaining Hold dwarves who still follow the gods and traditions of the Dwarven Empire from the Golden Age. They claim this makes them honourable, while others point out that such traditions were also followed by the eastern part of the Empire, which later became Infernal.

Seekers do not venerate stone and depth in the way of other dwarves, and have even been known to fight entirely without armour to cultivate a closer connection to the gods. The cult takes it upon itself to exact justice on oathbreakers, carrying out hunts and executions of which most Holds disapprove and yet turn a blind eye. In rarer cases, Seekers have been known to hunt outsiders deemed to have wronged a Hold in some way. This is a truly terrifying ordeal, for once the cult appoints a target, it will never stop seeking them until they are slain.

Truly your knowledge is dizzying. If those are Seekers, what is a Vengeance Seeker?

Oh. Ah…is that something separate? I mean, of course I know what it is. I'm just not inclined to divulge such information until I get a chance to do some more research.

What is the political structure of the Holds? Is each Hold an independent kingdom, or is there a single king?

The Dwarven Holds are very unusual in exhibiting a high level of cultural cohesion while remaining extremely independent both politically and geographically. Each Hold is a self-sufficient kingdom conducting its own military and economic affairs. There is no "high king", though alliances of various kinds are not uncommon between Holds, settled at lengthy and ceremonious moots. Cultural integration is maintained through trade, marriage exchange, and the activities of the Guild of Lorekeepers, which is the only guild to be somewhat unified across Holds.

Each Hold is a gerontocracy where power is held by the oldest representatives of each family, together forming various clans, each governed by thanes chosen by a single Hold monarch. The only currency of power recognised within the Holds is that of oaths and honour. An honourless leader does not need to be deposed – he or she will simply no longer be followed or obeyed.

Do the Holds have stronger relationships with some realms or species than others?

Dwarves have little care for outsiders, including the human nations closest to the White Mountains. Yet they occasionally assent to trade agreements or even military alliances when necessary. To the extent that they dabble in affairs of the wider world, they normally seek stability among the forces that surround them.

Like all peoples, dwarves have a natural distaste for various cultures beyond their own, but they are not quick to hatred against an entire species.

When they go to war, their target is normally a clear and singular enemy who has wronged them or who stands in the way of an important objective. Such forays can be overwhelming and brutal, leaving nothing behind but rubble.

Herr Sage, we must now ask the most important question of all. Tell us of dwarven cuisine. Do they really brew the strongest beer? Do they grow their own crops in the mountains or do they trade? What food is served at special events?

Truly, you strike at the heart of the Holds. Dwarves are master brewers indeed, and beer is universally consumed at events both special and mundane. Despite the claims of certain simpleminded professors, this is not the result of a special dwarven affinity for inebriation. The primary reason is that water is eschewed for lacking substance and solidity. Hence the legendary turgidity of dwarven ale.

The Guild of Brewers is one of the largest and most important guilds in any Hold, given special exemption from customs taxes and accorded a certain neutral status. The Guild's representatives are the only individuals allowed to come and go from a moot hall before agreement is reached, and the only dwarves not bound by that agreement. The Guild is responsible for the food and drink that allows all other parts of the Hold to function.

To acquire such victuals, in most Holds the Guild oversees terraced farms on the surface, with barley as the most essential crop, and mead hives also popular. Farmers are chosen for tolerance to open spaces, and are forced to adapt crops to the local environment, causing Hold diets to vary significantly. Where farming is not possible, food must be gathered or imported from other sources. Fungi and simple vegetables are sometimes cultivated underground, while rangers hunt meat both above and below.

Like their eastern cousins, Hold dwarves have become experts at finding ways to create a food surplus despite their geographical limitations. This makes dwarven cuisine hearty but often not particularly pleasant, I'm sorry to say.

EMPIRE OF SONNSTAHL

Sage, we wish to learn more of halflings. What is their place in the current era?

Halflings you say? Ah yes, excellent company over a glass or three. Some believe they used to have a fixed homeland, but I've never heard of one. In any case, they've become a fairly regular sight throughout Vetia, and well beyond, living in caravans and going from place to place, plying their trades. Many are specialist craftsmen, tailors and so forth.

With their natural wits and affable nature, halflings survive, and often prosper, largely by being useful and inoffensive. It's true they face more suspicion than welcome from the ignorant, but there's an old and fine pedigree to their culture, and what they don't know about the finer things in life is frankly not worth knowing. I get all my wine from old Funnygut on Via Gryphia – for a small fee I'll make an introduction.

Who defends the Beacons?

Wretched place, but I suppose it's a necessity. Soldiers returning from duty – the so-called Beaconers, known for their staring eyes – universally report unpleasant experiences. It's not just the worrisome threats emerging from the untamed East. The borderlands themselves are no place for decent folk.

The direct answer to your question is of course, the Emperor and the armies of Sonnstahl. The region is among the most militarised in the world. The many forts are supplied and coordinated by the fortress at Ostenfeste, where rules the knightly Order of the White Eye, which answers directly to the Imperial Palace in Aschau. It's a carbuncle of a place, swollen with passing patrols and legions of Inquisitorial agents. I can think of a few people I'd like to send there for an extended holiday. That idiot Finkle for a start, let's see how "noble" he finds the savages of the Steppe when they "step" out of his childish so-called books.

Does Emperor Matthias have a designated heir?

As a learned man I can talk with expertise on many topics, but the matter of Sonnstahl's succession is one about which I hold no opinions whatsoever. I can only relay the facts, Herr Inquisitor, whoops, I mean respected questioner.

Sonnstahl's Emperor does not designate an heir, since the role is not hereditary but appointed by a conclave of Electors. Of course, the natural heir is traditionally favoured – Matthias' Rothermeyer family has held the position for several generations now. Yet the laws of succession are complex throughout Vetia, and since Matthias is childless, it transpires that his natural heir would be a certain Princess Eleonore, daughter of the Equitan Mathilde the Wise and the Volskayan Wladyslaw the Cunning. This child Eleanor, a 16-year-old maiden, resides in Zmayevatz, the principality ruled by her childless aunt, and is, in theory at least, due to inherit four major Kingdoms. Needless to say, this situation represents enormous opportunity and danger for many factions across the continent.

There are other claimants, of course. Matthias' elder sister Josefa, despite her holy vows and declarations of political disinterest, is widely seen as a leading candidate, enjoying the support of many prelates and Electors. As a Daughter of Sunna, as such nuns are called, she's ineligible for imperial offices, but of course if she chose to step away from her duties in the Abbey, the situation would be greatly changed.

How common is the famous steam tank among Sonnstahl's armies?

Ah! The steam tanks, the Empire's most recent and notable military creation. The crowning glory of the Imperial Army. Of course they would have been built many years earlier if the Academy of Engineers had only accepted the notes I generously sent them without being solicited. But alas, so few recognise genius until it's too late. Thus today, for all the fanfare, there are yet only a small but growing number in active use – the exact figures are of course a military secret.

How are Sonnstahl's armies organised and trained? Locally or centrally?

The simple answer is both.

The Imperial Guard is selected from among the best of the many principalities, counties, baronies, free cities and other bishopries, and trained for the use of the Imperial Army – though it may, on occasion, be detached to a provincial task force. Meanwhile, the Provinces and Electors are required to provide a certain number of troops for the Emperor's use, and that means the bumpkins have to know the same drills. Thus, the Imperial Regulations Manual is used throughout the Empire.

Naturally, there are variations in certain techniques, philosophies and uniforms from region to region. Breidmark is known for horsemen, Scharland for marksmen, and Alfhaven for brawlers, for example.

HIGHBORN ELVES

Wise Sage, what is the relationship between the famous Arandai blademasters and the Masters of Canreig Tower?

We can forgive confusion in this case – many have failed to recognise the difference, especially since the remarkable sword masters are known by many other names: warrior aesthetes, blade poets and so forth. Their official title is the Paladins of Nab, a name which dates to their founding in the aftermath of the elves' civil war in the Third Age. Supposedly, the organisation was created as a new home for devotees of the War Crow after that goddess' public worship was shunned, and proceeded to focus on the beauty within the craft of death. Once scorned, these artists were eventually welcomed into the Pearl Throne's armies and are now considered exemplars of Arandai skill.

Canrac, meanwhile, is an unrelated academic institution. But certain of its greatest leaders – those who seek the secrets of perfect balance between the three natures of elven spirit – have adopted the blades and fighting styles of the sword masters. Hence the source of confusion.

Can you cast some light on the special relationship that seems to exist between the Arandai and dragons?

There are few pairings in the world better aligned than that of the dragons of Rymâ and the lords and ladies of Celeda Ablan. Long lived, aloof, inscrutable, proud and dedicated to an endless pursuit of knowledge and riches, it would appear the gods made them perfect for each other. Perhaps there is some truth to old Myerdink's theory that the elves' original settlement of the White Isles, home to the largest concentration of dragons in the world, was more than just coincidence.

Even while partnerships between dragons and Arandai are by no means a common occurrence, the sheer number of potential encounters means the Pearl Throne can count upon draconic assistance beyond comparison. This bond appears to be growing with each generation, as more and more elves and Rymân dragons come to see the two societies as part of an interwoven whole. The thought of such a union has kept many mortal lords awake at night. On the other hand, even elves cannot hope to fully understand the inscrutable motivations of such ancient creatures – and there can be grave consequences for relying on misguided assumptions.

Are the forces of the Highborn organised and recruited by the central government or by individual lords?

According to intelligence retrieved by Field Marshal Haas, the armed forces of the Arandai Empire are a mix of levy citizen soldiers, feudal formations and lifelong professionals. While the various regiments have individual commanders, the armies are more uniform than most mortal nations. Highborn are expected to serve for set periods over their long lives, resulting in a gradual rotation of troops and an almost uniformly trained and battle-ready population. Teaching, equipment and uniforms are all provided by the Queen's government.

Sage, what is the political situation of the Arandai Empire following its troubles in Sagarika and the rise of new powers in the Ninth Age?

In spite of the incident caused by ambassador Renouge, Avrasi envoys have managed to return with valuable information, and fairly ill tidings I'm afraid.

The Pearl Throne has indeed suffered setbacks, and since the turn of the century the Isolationist faction has dominated court politics in Aldan.

But it would be very misguided to see the Highborn as an empire in decline, as I have repeatedly and fruitlessly tried to explain to the Senate. Arandai strength is as great as ever, and unfortunately reports indicate that they may soon be willing to use it.

Maritime colonial ventures by human powers in recent decades have been noticed by the elves' Royal Navy, and the beast of the White Isles has started to stir. The Imperialist faction is in the ascendant, with growing calls for retribution against those who believe they can share the seas with Celeda Ablan. Worst of all, the new Queen appears willing to heed these calls, and has found a loophole that allows her to unleash her personal guard in the field beyond the White Isles.

Do the Arandai face threats in the White Isles themselves? Are there feral tribes or darker powers there?

In general, no. The White Isles are sufficiently remote that they were likely uninhabited by intelligent species when the elves first found them, with the exception of dragons. The Arandai have worked hard to keep them that way, though not with perfect success – a recent if brief vermin infestation at a naval base proved quite an embarrassment, for example, while a colony of various kinds of scraplings from some ill-fated ogre expedition is rumoured to persist in the eastern marshes. The islands are large, of course, and not all tamed. The dangers of the wilderness lurk in many areas, including strange and terrible wild creatures quite unrelated to the dragons.

Additionally, elves are not immune to the temptations of the Dark Gods, which can cause serious damage from time to time, as in all advanced societies. While elves cannot succumb to vampirism, there have been unsubstantiated rumours of tribes of undead Highborn haunting the most remote islands, fuelled by foul necromancy – courtesy, perhaps, of one of their deranged mages who finally went too far.

INFERNAL DWARVES

There are shifting relationships between the many Infernal Citadels. Which Citadels are more friendly to each other and which are rivals?

Such alliances do indeed shift, I'm given to understand, and can change quickly with new leadership in a certain Citadel. Intelligence about politics on the Blasted Plain is hard to come by, even for one as well-informed as I, but it's clear that the main rivalries of recent years have emerged between the Citadels connected to the Steel Road, such as Kubnut Bebit and Lortikash, and the Citadels that aren't, like Gar Shakhub and Sakumesh.

Zalaman Tekash and its sister Citadel Zetivak, which are on the line, typically attempt to remain neutral in most disputes, hoping to retain their de facto "capital" status without appearing so strong that they risk a united opposition.

What is the relationship between Hold dwarves and Infernal dwarves? Are they enemies? Or do they respect each other since they are the same species?

You recall, of course, that both powers are heirs of the ancient Dwarven Empire, divided by vehement and unforgotten accusations of betrayal during the Ages of Ruin. Their cultures, both built upon a foundation of sworn and sealed oaths and the bearing of grudges, are ill-equipped for reconciliation, rendered all the more difficult by mutual condemnation; Hold dwarves shun what they see as the reckless and lazy usage of sorcery and servants; Infernal dwarves sneer at what they call weakness and cowardly isolationism.

Nevertheless, since re-establishing contact in the Ninth Age, the two cultures have not come into conflict especially more often than they have with other powers. Emissaries and traders have been exchanged, although so have occasional invasion forces. Some say that while each hates much about the other, they share a mutual dislike of non-dwarves who seek to paint either dwarven faction as malicious or greedy.

All in all, the relationship has shifted over the years to the extent that I would not want to categorise it as any one thing – especially when you remember that neither group operates as a single, centralised power. Individual Holds and Citadels are perfectly capable of maintaining their own feuds and alliances that have nothing to do with the rest of their people.

I've heard that the Inferno is a portal to Hell. Is it true that the Infernal Dwarves are all in league with the Dark Gods?

Absolutely not. This myth has been perpetuated by too many so-called scholars and needs to be put to bed. The Infernal dwarves value the trappings of civilisation as much as we do – theirs is a society of strict hierarchies, unforgiving laws and firm political structures: everything that the Dark Gods seek to tear asunder. Moreover, the Infernal culture is deeply religious. They are devoted to the gods of their land, a pantheon, known as the Vaneb, which is entirely unaffiliated with Hell or the Dark Gods – despite the profusion of fiery imagery!

Like any people, there are those among the Infernals who have succumbed to the forbidden worship of the Seven, but they are just as ruthlessly hunted by taurukh officers and spymasters as their counterparts in Vetia are hunted by the Inquisition.

Finally I should point out that while the Veil is extremely thin at the Inferno, it is not in fact a portal to Hell. While any area of sufficiently high magic can be crossed by supernals, including daemons of the Seven, the region in the vicinity of the Inferno is more often used by creatures affiliated with the Vaneb – those we call kadim.

Do Infernal dwarves trade with every other faction? Or are there some who are too vile, even for them?

The Infernal dwarves have shown little compunction about the methods with which they enrich themselves, and exhibit no shame in their choice of trading partners. Much more often it is they who are rebuffed – only the most unscrupulous or desperate Vetians will dare to deal with them, and even some goblins and vermin refuse to meet, thanks to their reputation as slavers and vassal-makers.

KINGDOM OF EQUITAINE

What are the Fey? Are there different kinds aligned with Equitaine and the sylvan elves?

It's true, "Fey" is a word used to describe different categories of being. Elves of all types are often called Fey, though they are mortal (if very long-lived) creatures from this Realm.

In the context of Equitaine, the Fey are supernal creatures of many kinds, hailing from the Immortal Realm and aligned with the goddess commonly called the Lady, worshipped by Equitans.

Other supernals, especially woodland creatures allied with the sylvans, are also called Fey sometimes, although we educated folk are more likely to use terms like Forest Spirits. The sylvan Fey are magical beings who may or may not be aligned with the elven gods; typically their first care is the forest itself. Most seem to operate as somewhat free agents, allying with the sylvans out of choice.

Who are the serjeants of the ordos?

The ordos of Equitaine are often compared to the clergy of other nations, and it's true that they are religious – but they are more diverse than, for example, the church of Sunna. Each ordo has its own special interests and trades, and is sponsored by its own lord.

"Serjeants" is a collective term commonly used for the military agents of an ordo – those who are trained to fight. Usually their task is to defend ordo estates from beasts or brigands, but such warriors can also be called to battle when needed.

What lives in Sague and why isn't it settled by Equitaine?

Sague is a wide realm stretching across the middle of the Kingdom. I must correct your misapprehension: it is most certainly controlled and settled by the Equitans. Owing to the treacherous, craggy terrain, there is not much good farmland in Sague, and its population is much smaller than other regions in Equitaine, especially the South. It therefore has a reputation as something of a wilderness, and it's true that you'll find more wild beasts and outlaw camps out there than in the more civilised parts of the country.

But Sague still enjoys the King's protection and it's by no means entirely lawless. There are several impressive castles and fortifications within the region, and many small towns have thrived there, especially those along the highways that connect northern and southern cities.

How does an Equitan paladin differ from a Sonnstahler inquisitor?

They are the same in that both groups would be highly offended by the question! And because I must choose my words carefully to avoid their attention.

Both inquisitors and paladins are responsible for seeking out corrupting elements that attempt to remain hidden within the heart of upstanding communities. Primarily, that means the agents of the Dark Gods and of blood-drinking Night Lords.

However, they are two quite different kinds of organisation. Paladins technically belong to the

Ordo Paladia – a loose association that dates from the time of Uther. They are theoretically apolitical, but many have close ties to damsels, and some report to the King. In many respects they are simply individual knights who have pledged to root out evil. The Inquisition, meanwhile, is the largest wing of the sprawling Church of Sunna, administered from the Curia of the Supreme Prelate in Reva, with jurisdiction across all of Sonnstahl and Destria, as well as most of Arcalea and occasionally beyond. It is a vast, bureaucratic spy-ring, and a top-down infrastructure.

Who are the Sainted and what sort of powers and abilities do they possess?

Ah, the Saints of Equitaine, about whom songs are sung, canvasses are painted and glass is stained. A Sainted knight is one who has completed a true quest and has been offered the Lady's cup to drink from. I should note that Equitans get very cross if you make lewd jokes about the Lady's cup, as I am sorry to say I have learned from experience.

In any case, empowered by the Lady, Sainted individuals have shown a variety of skills. Most are braver and stronger than mortal humans, and more powerful in combat. Some know spells or other magics, or wield enchanted weaponry. Such elevated individuals are at least partially supernal – they are said to join the Lady's court, which implies that they can visit the Immortal Realm. I'm not so predisposed to believe such tales as gullible oafs like Lemagne, but given that they can live for centuries, I must admit the evidence is in his favour, even if his latest paper is self-serving drivel.

OGRE KHANS

What is the relationship between ogres and scraplings? Are the scraplings slaves or do they serve willingly? If so, is it out of a sense of cooperation or is it just for the sake of survival?

Who's to say what manner of creatures dwell in the great expanses of Augea, or their relationship with the mighty khans of flesh and coin?

I am, for this is no fresh-faced undergraduate to whom you speak, this is a paragon of scholarship, famed throughout the...well you know the spiel by now. Scraplings are not a species, as many ignoramuses believe. They are a category of employment, a label bestowed on any creature who serves the khans for gold or protection. In the most savage tribes, they may be closer to indentured thralls or even slaves, but the majority of khans are pleased to treat their scraplings as faithful retainers, especially among the mountain ogres, who know no higher philosophy than that of debt and restitution, and always pay what is owed.

On the steppe, the relationship is perhaps more akin to symbiosis. In return for food and safety, they perform minor duties, largely undirected and even unnoticed, including the vital service of clean up. Scraplings may see themselves, or be seen, as scraps – the remnants of other groups and cultures – and they survive on the (rather copious) scraps from the ogres' tables. Many scraplings take familiar forms, but the job is also known to be carried out by stranger creatures, such as the ice gremlins of the Sky Mountains and the rarely seen kobold archivists of eastern Augea.

There are ogre-ruled states in the Sagarikadesha. Have these clashed with the plague cult of the vermin?

The rodent Cult of Errahman does not typically control territory, as this question perhaps assumes, preferring to convert pre-existing populations using either persuasion or, in our darkest hour, military force. Nevertheless, you are correct that the plague cult is highly active in the Desha where it was born – a vast land where many different peoples and species have carved out their own fiefdoms. Conflict between Sagarikan ogres and vermin (both Caelysian and Errahmite) has certainly been documented over the years – the most notable case involved the poisoning of an important feast that provoked the khans to a terrible fury. However, I'm not aware of any special or enduring rivalry between the two.

Which cultures use ogres as mercenaries? Why are they not seen in any other armies?

Not seen in other armies? Whatever can you mean!? Ogre mercenaries have frequently appeared among the armies of almost all nations, cultures and lords – most famously the Iron Crowns of the Middle Sea. Of course, being outsiders, and sellswords, such ogres are hardly likely to be mentioned by anyone cataloguing the traditional military forces of the great powers, as I have attempted to explain to that unmentionable dullard Lockheimer from the Theoretical Zoology faculty on multiple occasions.

I have heard of two ogre cultures: the nomadic tribes of the steppe and those fortifying the mountains. Are these the only ones?

This is something of a simplification, but nevertheless it holds a degree of truth: those are the primary cultures and largest ogre populations. There are, however, many other ogres cultures – most are offshoots of these two, but a rare few are independent and quite different.

Within Vetia, there are the regimental ogres, answering to the so-called Belly Captain, who oversees the laws of mercenary engagement from his den of villainy in southern Glauca. There are the ogres enslaved by the Infernal Dwarves, many of whom dream of freedom and rebuilding the legendary Akhanate of ages past. There is a sizeable native population in Silexia, who are said to maintain ties to their cousins on the Augean steppe via irregular and extremely dangerous treks across the polar ice cap. Other ogre bands can be found in small numbers all around the globe, usually in the form of traders, bodyguards or bandits. On rare occasions, some have even taken to sea aboard their employers' vessels, or commandeered ships of their own.

Are there any important sites or settlements that are to be steamrolled by the expanding Steel Road?

Even such a fount of insight as me is not familiar with the Infernals' expansion plans for the Steel Road railway, which they preserve as a paramount secret. Some observers doubt such plans even exist, at least in the Sky Mountains. Having completed the route to Tsuandan, it's likely that the dwarves will turn next to a western route, since further branches to the east would yield diminishing returns. This would leave the mountain ogres free to focus their efforts on sabotaging the currently existing line, and undercutting its prices with new routes along the older Silk Roads, rather than fending off further work teams supported by large armies from the Blasted Plain.

ORCS AND GOBLINS

Orcs demonstrate behaviour progression with age. How long does a freshly hatched "feral" orc take to become a "veteran" or an "iron" orc?

Don't listen to charlatans who claim to have established the definitive timeline for an orcish lifecycle. The truth is that an orc's maturity is not measured in years but in combat – orcs do not remember when they were born, but they remember their first battle. The maturing process also requires the presence of a larger tribe. An orc brood integrated into a tribe in its infancy and shown the ways of battle will grow, mentally at least, much faster than an orc brood lost in the wild for years. Like humans, orcs learn maturity; it doesn't come naturally. Until it finds its tribe, a brood can remain feral indefinitely.

The transition to "iron" status is somewhat more subtle, depending again on how much fighting an orc survives, as well as how rapidly its brood shrinks in size, and the availability of other iron orcs to act as guides.

Incidentally, another factor that has made it very difficult to establish orcs' biological lifespan is that almost none have been known to die of old age.

Could a greenskin walk freely in other societies, or would they be arrested or executed?

First of all, "greenskin" is inaccurate; while many Warborn do demonstrate green pigmentation, the full spectrum incorporates all shades of browns, yellows, greys and more. As to their ability to enter other societies – this varies greatly from place to place. Individual goblins manage to find a place almost anywhere, as their cleverness in providing useful service – as well as their skill in pretending that they don't report back to their worldwide espionage ring – knows no bounds.

Orcs are a tougher proposition. In small numbers, they can be seen going unmolested in the most metropolitan parts of the world – I noticed a pair at the Candiano Taverna last week. Such sightings are very rare, not because of the hostility they may face, but because orcs almost never choose to leave their brood, and a whole brood is cause for concern everywhere.

Are orcs and goblins nomadic? Do they have settlements? Do they farm?

Orcs are universally nomadic, goblins almost always sedentary. The smaller Warborn live in botanical cities commonly called Gardens, kept carefully hidden from the outside world using miraculous forms of camouflage, or by locating them in difficult-to-reach areas such as caves or forests. They don't farm in the conventional sense, but they do grow a vast quantity and variety of exotic plants throughout their living areas, as a central part of their culture.

Why don't orcs use more technology? Surely that would allow them to dish out more pain.

Nomads are rarely able to develop advanced technology, and this is doubly true for orcs, whose lifespans are shortened by frequent risk of death in battle. Many orcs do exhibit an instinctive interest in craftwork, making cunning weapons and armours to improve their prowess in combat, and mature orcs are known for developing fairly impressive blacksmithing skills.

You must remember that the orcish love of fighting is a mysterious, deep-rooted drive quite unknown to civilised people. They could never value technology or art in the same way we do, because such concerns rarely improve their mental or social wellbeing. Having said this, they do frequently adorn themselves in paints and scrimshaw totems.

Do orcs and goblins worship gods?

Indeed they do. Orcs and goblins have two separate religions and pantheons reflecting their separate natures, but both are based on a unifying Warborn "principle" called Wapaka by orcs and Goga by goblins. This divine essence reveals a richer and more complex religious epistemology than that seen in many cultures, much as the blinkered priests and prelates try to deny it. It's made even harder to follow when you understand that goblin initiates ("gogtuk") have a different comprehension of such matters to that of other goblins.

Orcish gods embody Wakapa and are called the Apajik, or Victorious Ones. They include Tazrek, Zagjan and Krajuk, gods of chieftanship, sport and crafting respectively.

Goblin gods, the Hamikish, or Free Ones, embody Goga. They include Mikinok, Kishirik, and Hiba-Re, gods of innovation, ambition and assassination. And most important of all: Kuruka, the Twin God of cunning and death.

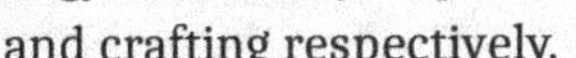

SAURIAN ANCIENTS

What do we know of the Saurian Empire of the Dawn Age?

Almost nothing for certain. Most scholars believe it should more accurately be called the Anurarch Empire, since saurian society as we see it today did not yet exist. But even this is an educated guess.

All we have are the primordial myths from dozens of cultures, along with the ruined remains of edifices and installations that can be found around the world. These stories typically speak of reptilian tyrants who enslaved all other species with the aid of unfathomable magics, until their primary base of power was destroyed by a Cataclysm caused by a falling comet or star. The peoples of the world subsequently rose up to annihilate the hated mage-emperors, ushering in the Second Age.

Is it true that anurarchs are never seen without their inferior servants?

Within the saurians' Collaboration – those enclaves that cooperate in a single worldwide polity – anurarchs are indeed always accompanied by warriors. But contrary to what fools like the Chair of Sapient Herpetology have claimed, these warriors are most likely not the anurarchs' subordinates at all.

Owing to their amoral nature and fiendish intelligence, anurarchs are not trusted by the Collaboration, so they are kept under permanent watch to prevent them attempting any nefarious schemes. True scholars like myself, therefore, believe their retinues of warriors are in fact jailors. Of course, even among the saurians there is likely some debate about whether such measures are sufficient – anurarchs may be so wily that they are able to scheme even in captivity. But their great power makes the risk worth it, for they are often willing to aid the saurians in battle and other endeavours – perhaps to curry favour as part of some ineffable long-game.

We've heard that some saurians are powerful Diviners – how is that possible when the heathens have no gods?

Ah, I must correct a crucial misunderstanding here. The Path of Divination is a form of magic that allows wizards to see far and know much, but despite the etymology, it is not strictly related to the divine. A mage need not have an affiliation to any deity to pursue this Path – unlike the Path of Thaumaturgy, which draws directly on the power of the gods.

Is it true that saurians share some kind of communal bond? How does such a thing operate?

A fascinating question, with more than a few theories currently in contention. Observers have long noted the saurians' ability to seemingly act as one on the field, going to battle in eerie silence without drummers, flags or shouted commands, and yet responding to each other with uncanny simultaneity.

Many have ignorantly attributed this to an insectoid hive-mind. The idea of such a single collective will must be discounted. For one thing, no "queen" or central directing force has ever been found. For another, interrogations reveal that each saurian is an intelligent individual, fully capable of self-direction when removed from her society.

Certain zoologists have made convincing claims that the saurian bond is mediated by a sonic signal so high or low-pitched that it's undetectable to other species. The effect appears to be largely instinctive and emotional – it cannot communicate complex information, only simple feelings. Enough to provide forewarning of danger, to perhaps calm soldiers in battle, or to allow for silent coordination of pre-established strategies.

Our saurian captives refuse to identify any kind of military or political leaders. How can their armies and society function without leadership?

The previous answer provides a solution to the practical functioning of such a situation. Leadership is not so essential when soldiers can sense each other directly.

But the saurian disdain for kings and gods runs deeper. Partly, it results from their Vitalist philosophy – concerned with abstract notions of life, energy and entropy, against which political power is a petty and unnecessary affair.

And partly, I believe, it's simply a facet of their culture, which is thought to have developed over millennia on the remote island of Atua, entirely free of war. Who's to say if lust for power would dissipate from any species in such conditions – even our own?

But enough of hypotheticals – the main thing to remember about saurians is that they are not like us. Their ways of thinking about things we take for granted – society, hierarchies, symbols, and so forth – are often absent or completely alien to our own. No matter how much we learn about them, they will forever remain the strangest and most enigmatic of people.

SYLVAN ELVES

Oh Savage Sage! There are ghosts in the trees, and more than just knife-ears. The trees seem to think in ways they ought not to, and have become vengeful. Our mages taste the aspect of the supernal on them, but they do not seem to be direct agents of the elven gods, unlike the daemons of the Seven or the kadim from the Flame. Do they simply ally with the elves out of mutual convenience and respect, or was a deal struck? Who leads these fractious tree daemons, if anything at all?

Consensus has not yet been reached concerning the precise nature of the walking trees, though that hasn't stopped many brainless upstarts from proclaiming their theories. The most plausible premise is that while these beings may have origins among supernals who entered this realm in the Cataclysm of the Dawn Age, those we see today are merely their descendants: creatures who have merged with the physical realm and become simply magical beings rather than immortals. The very oldest trees of the forest may be an exception, if we are to believe claims that they have endured since ancient times, growing only more ornery and knotted with the ages.

Whatever they are, they have allied with the sylvans since time immemorial. The origins of this union are lost to the ages, but it was surely forged on the shared instinct to nurture and defend the woods.

We know of no formal leadership among the treekin. But the strongest spirits do seem to have a paternal role, guiding their youngers – much as great minds like myself serve as mentors to more feeble scholars within the savage realm of academia.

Are the sylvans the original elves?

Indeed. All elven histories agree that their people began in the woods – not yet called sylvan but simply elves. While later migrations and exploration took their species to new shores and produced new cultures, the forest fae have changed little over the many ages. The Highborn and Daeb call them primitive for that reason, while the sylvans see themselves as having stayed faithful to the true path, the spiritual balance and connection with the nurturing forest. You can read all about it in my book *If You Go Down To The Woods Today* – I'll give you half price if you buy direct from me.

What threatens the forest?

Their power may be great, but the elves of the forest face as many if not more threats than the rest of us. Some believe that humans were permitted to settle near their woods as a bulwark against greater dangers. If that's true, the policy may have backfired: today, the encroachment of urban and manufacturing powers is a great concern for sylvans throughout the world. Though of course, by no means all such powers are human. Additionally, sylvans are prey to the depredations of the Dark Gods, Vermin, Warborn and so on, just as we are.

Is it true that Sylvan Elves have the most grievances against dwarves (nasty tree cutters), the beast herds (dark children of the wild) and malevolent forest spirits?

Sylvans have long memories and it's quite likely they have continued to distrust dwarvenkind ever since the wars of the Golden Age. Conflict with the beast herds is also well established, though this is probably just a matter of proximity, since beasts are among the only other creatures who sometimes seek to live in the deepest woods. In truth, the herds' approach to nature is perhaps closer to the sylvans' than most others. It's unclear if there are any special rivalries here – personally I would guess that the fae have equal dislike for most external powers, all of which have caused them grief on a more or less regular basis over the centuries.

Regarding malevolent forest spirits – it's hard to tell whether these exist, since most forest spirits appear malevolent to human reporters. But it's quite likely that not all forest life is perfectly attuned to sylvan civilisation. Some may avoid or oppose it. Perhaps the elves treat such creatures much as we would dangerous wild animals – after all, the fae have never sought to make the forests perfectly tame or safe.

UNDYING DYNASTIES

Who poses the greatest threat to the Napteshi dynasties?

The answer is themselves. Naptesh is perhaps not one dynasty but two, locked in civil war since the Age of Death. When Queen Teput and the usurper Setesh slew each other at the end of the Second Age, both survived in undead form to lead their respective factions for the rest of eternity in the smouldering struggle for Naptesh's soul. Though each side's fortunes have risen and fallen over the centuries, today the Queen still rules most of the holy necropolises along the Sacred River, while the Great Jackal's stronghold lies in the wastes of western Hassar.

The kingdom of Naptesh also faces external threats – human, elf and other raiders and invaders both from across the seas, and from Taphrian kingdoms, all seeking the legends of Napteshi gold and arcane secrets. The Vampire Covenant is particularly covetous of such treasures, as are some of the Dark Gods and various barbarian species. But such concerns must seem trivial and fleeting to a kingdom that has stood for millennia.

How has the state of undeath affected the society of Naptesh? What do Napteshi farmers do now for example?

An undying kingdom has little need for farmers, or any other trades besides those of bone and spirit. The souls of Naptesh slumber through the ages, no longer troubled by the needs or desires of mortals. When their kingdom needs them, they are channelled into skeleton or stone, and rise to defend the land.

There remain small populations of living Napteshi who travel the desert in scattered nomadic tribes. Once they are consecrated to the kingdom, their souls join the undead legions upon their death. In life, they provide other services, such as the collection of fresh corpses for use by said legions. Some even act as agents of the mystical Order of the Rising Sun.

Can an undying dynasty increase its numbers, or is it limited to the original number of soldiers?

It depends on what created the dynasty in the first place. As just discussed, in some cases it's possible for living people to mark their souls as participants in whatever curse or calamity prevents the dynasty from crossing the Veil to a normal afterlife. In this way, a dynasty can indeed grow, but only if it can find people willing to undergo such devotion!

Was the first vampire a Napteshi mortal?

No. Whatever your prelate is telling you,
vampires have existed since before any recorded
kingdom or empire. Some say they are as old as
humanity itself. Naptesh may be the oldest of the
great human nations, but our species itself
(and its blood-drinking parasite) is much
older!

**Why do undying armies bring their
hierophants to battle instead of hiding
them?**

An interesting question, and one I have
debated with those who charmingly call
themselves my colleagues. Some believe it
is a matter of range – a necromantic
specialist is required to maintain the
bindings of the undead in the vicinity. It
remains unclear, however, if the concept
of distance can be applied to such
esoteric phenomena.

My personal belief is that, at least in the
case of Naptesh, the priests and mages
of the dead accompany their armies in
order to impress their foes with the
strength and glory of their gods. In
other words, their pride is too great to
permit them to cower in safety, even
if they are a liability on the
battlefield.

VAMPIRE COVENANT

Other than Gilles of Equitaine, who is the greatest, most feared, historically best known vampire?

The trouble with a question like this is that vampires may come to hear of anything we discuss, and they are full of wrathful pride. In such respects they resemble the gods they so hate. Out of caution, therefore, I will not name a single "greatest" vampire – the Lecturer in Heretical History tried that last term, not long before they found him strapped to the roof with all the blood drained from his body.

Instead, I will mention the founders of the bloodlines known to exist today. Those would be Gilles for Sangreal, as you already seem to know. Then there's Evadne of Myra for the Lamians, and the Venerable Rishalu for the Vetala. All three are thought to be currently dead, at least officially – I'd say it's a safe bet that at least some of them are active under other names or guises. The identity of the founder of the Strigoi, who have existed since the Dawn Age, has been lost to history.

Can a vampire appear human to a casual observer? Could they infiltrate normal society?

Indeed they can: this is their chief and most famous ability. It is a trifling thing for a vampire to apply a glamour that shows the face of a fair and living human – although the effect can normally be stripped away by application of a mirror.

The Strigoi disdain such subterfuge, but all other bloodlines use this skill as a matter of course. They work together within the

Ask The Sage

Covenant, a secret society dedicated to infiltrating and controlling humanity without ever revealing itself. Thus, vampires are, above all else, spies and dissemblers.

What long-term goals would a vampire have, other than to rule and enslave others? What are they working towards?

A question that has troubled our species from its earliest days. The sorry truth is that no one knows for sure. As mentioned, the Covenant itself has the apparent goal of ruling and puppeting human powers in secret. But it is an organisation defined by its excessively labyrinthine layers of duplicity. Its intentions are hidden behind motives inside objectives within deep and unfathomable purposes. Perhaps even its highest initiates cannot say for certain what its real goals are, if it even has any. And remember, each vampire has his or her own schemes which may diverge from Covenant orthodoxy.

Whatever the truth of the Covenant's motivations, you can be sure that whenever a conspiracy is uncovered within the highest echelons of power, more often than not there will be vampires at the heart of it.

Where do vampires come from; how is a new vampire born? How does its power as a vampire relate to its power before becoming a vampire?

Ah, the undead birds and the blood-sucking bees. You see, when two vampires become amorous...apologies, I couldn't resist. Vampires are in fact created by a brutal and usually non-consensual exchange of blood between a human and an existing vampire, known as siring. After death, the victim's soul gradually fuses with the matter of its body, a transformation that grants immortality along with the other strengths and weaknesses displayed by vampires – and also awakens the Thirst. It is said that through a truly titanic application of will, a fledgling vampire might resist the Thirst in those early nights,

which allows its soul to depart peacefully across the Veil. Almost all victims, however, succumb.

Of course, the other way to become a vampire is to conduct a ritual of such massive sorcerous power and transgression that one seizes the Thirst for oneself, creating a new bloodline. Many have attempted this method, but vanishingly few have succeeded. The failure of the ritual means death – or in the rarest and strangest cases, lich-hood.

A newly created vampire retains the knowledge, skills and memories of its mortal persona, though typically these pale in comparison to the abilities and hungers it has gained.

Are all vampires human, or can there also be vampires from other species?

Strange to say, but only humans can become vampires. Despite the facile theories offered by the likes of Sub-Dean Klarmann, the reason for this is not fully understood.

It's said that vampires can be resurrected even long after being slain. What is the longest known time that a vampire has stayed dead before returning?

The record for vampiric resurrection is more than two thousand years (approximately, depending on whose chronology you follow), when Zegrath of Lish, who was exposed to sunlight in the Third Age, was encountered and killed again by Queen Genoveva at the start of the Ninth Age.

The record is of course contested and impossible to verify for certain. In many cases, proof of life is hard to establish, because vampires may attempt to hide their resurrection by taking new identities. Proof of death is equally tricky, as it is fairly simple to falsify a vampire's demise. Still, there is more than enough proof that almost nothing can keep a vampire dead forever.

VERMIN SWARM

Herr Selig, how can the people ignore the existence of the Vermin menace?

I wouldn't let the Inquisition hear that kind of talk. Official doctrine holds that vermin power was irrevocably broken by the Goddess, and to suggest that it still exists is to suggest that Her divine power has limits.

Naturally, there are many who are well aware of the, ahem, somewhat overstated nature of such dogma, especially among educated scholars like you and I. I suspect the combination of Sunnan scripture's emphasis on the total defeat of the vermin, together with the vermin's own varied and ingenious methods to avoid detection have conspired to keep the full scope of their power obscured from most human eyes. Almost everyone is aware that rats still lurk under the earth, and companies of mercenary "exterminators" can even be hired to root them out. But very few know the complete and terrible truth.

Why does the Cult of Errahman go to battle alongside the rodents' senatorial army? Especially if, as rumoured, the Senate assassinated Barbas, their prophet!

Like all cults, the pestilent followers of Errahman have proven prone to schism. According to Kleperaus' latest dispatches from Near Augea, while the Errahmites believe fanatically in the supremacy of their god, ascendant factions still cherish the ideals of Avrasi heritage, and are willing to defend the state against external threats even as they campaign to overthrow the religious order. The prime goal of the Cult is the conversion of new followers; Kleperaus believes it hopes to gain popularity and political advantage from aiding the legions.

Meanwhile, there are plenty of ambitious would-be consuls in the Senate who have recognised the growing plebeian power of the Cult and are all too happy to risk the disfavour of the patrician class in order to court it. This only brings the Errahmites further into the fold as they begin to find footholds in the Senate itself.

How do you explain incorrect use of Avrasi terms by the Vermin? Don't they call themselves Avrasi?

This may surprise some, especially that fool Fitzburg, but the Swarm is not the true culture of Avras, despite its many determined claims. Vermin merely ape the styles and fashions of the ancients – they are not the ancients themselves. For goodness sake – some of them apparently feel that a mere wooden triangle on top of a staff is enough to symbolise the mighty Avrasi aquilas. Their continuous mistakes and misunderstandings of classical culture and terminology is a famous source of amusement for the educated observer.

We've heard reference to a "Ratking" distinct from their seeming leader. Could I prevail upon you to clarify?

You're correct that the legendary "Ratking" is quite distinct from the very real Rat Kings who ruled Avras before the coming of Sunna. The single-word term is supposedly taken from the phenomenon of regular small rats found with their tails entangled. Certain ancient and esoteric sources have suggested that the Vermin were originally created by such an occurrence, charged with spellcraft from beyond the Veil. The result was said to be a bizarre monstrosity comprised of dozens of connected rodents, which developed a singular, crazed and telepathic consciousness.

Some have claimed that this Ratking still endures, tended by an organisation so clandestine that even the Vermin themselves are unaware of its existence or influence – an organisation that secretly works to put the monster's schemes for devouring the world slowly and patiently into action. Of course, since those making such claims are always found to be insane, I have never paid them any mind.

I was told that Dusk Senators contrive to disdain plebeians and fight tyrants as part of the same creed. How do you explain such a contradiction?

You see, the Dusk Senate has long seen itself as a bulwark against kings and masters, seeking to eliminate any who would subjugate Avras to the power of a single *rex* – though they're not always successful, of course. And yet these assassins still see themselves as senators, albeit of a secretive variety, and thus highly ranked and worthy nobles of Vermin society, far above the filthy, teeming mob. Dusk Senators are far from apolitical, of course, and can be cajoled, bribed or persuaded like anyone else to support certain figures or even bend their definition of tyranny.

Some say that certain vermin distinguish themselves by the colour of their fur. Do they intentionally breed to achieve such distinctions?

Professor Sorrenti from the Arcane Zoology department would have you think so, as would his ill-begotten disciples. But the evidence shows that Vermin prefer to use dye to bring their pelts to the desired colours. Still, it may be true that some colours are incentivised by natural selection. A red-furred vermin who appears unwounded when he bleeds in battle may gain a reputation for strength, allowing him to gather more food and become indeed stronger. A vermin with especially dark black fur may inspire more fear, again improving his chances of success in life.

WARRIORS OF THE DARK GODS

Where does Hellforged armour come from?

Not from Hell, as its overexcitable namers suggest. A Warrior's distinctive armour is made of ordinary iron, which it seems they themselves must provide to a daemon capable of forging it into an eldritch steel. Such a process likely takes place in the Mortal Realm, since mundane materials cannot normally survive in the ineffable lands of the Immortal. Daemons can be conjured almost anywhere, although meeting them in or near the Wasteland is common for Warriors who can reach such a destination.

While the title of Warrior is gained when one swears the Pact, promising one's soul to a Dark God, many Warriors feel they are "incomplete" until they have acquired their armour – a significant rite of passage on the Paths of Ascension.

Can Hellforged armour be taken as a trophy and worn by those who don't worship the Dark Gods?

Perhaps, if the taker was the right fit! But likely not by normal mortals. Such armour is absurdly heavy – even the strongest humans, elves and dwarves would struggle to fight under such weight. The stuff is intended to be worn only by those who have been empowered specifically to wear it. Nor would many desire to clothe themselves in the symbol of such a hated foe.

So yes it can serve as a fine trophy – I was told that Colonel Stoltenberg nailed a suit of Warrior armour to the front of a steam tank at the Battle of Hannawald. But it's less likely to be useful for practical apparel.

How do Warriors build a working community, in terms of food, supplies, shelter and keeping wild creatures as battle mounts?

Kadovich was lauded for his paper on barbarian economies earlier this year, even though his arguments were so poorly informed as to be barely worth the parchment they were printed on. The truth is, whatever the religious types may say, that there is no magical source of the Warrior's wealth – no daemons leaving crates of food, no mana raining down to grow the warbands, no palaces left ready-furnished for the Warrior's comfort.

A band of Warriors makes its way the same as any nomadic tribe – living off the land and off its livestock, sometimes trading with outsiders and so forth. Each Warrior is expected to provide for him or herself, carrying whatever they require, and taking whatever they need. If they run out of food, they starve. If they lack skins to make tents, they freeze. Warriors are hardier than most, and they are by no means easy prey for wild beasts or the elements. But they are still mortal.

The advantage Warriors have that other nomads lack is strength of arms. Most of a Warrior's material goods are won by violent raids, or tributes demanded in place of raids. Some warbands have become impressively wealthy by such methods.

How do Warriors view daemons and vice versa?

The illiterate masses – by which I mean the staff room – often see Warriors and daemons as perfectly aligned. The two are practically conflated as a single force, if you listen to the spiel of clerics and even poets. In truth, while they share the same masters and the same attitude towards civilisation, the mortal and immortal followers of the Dark Gods are quite different in many of their goals and behaviours.

Warriors are said to think first and foremost of themselves, seeking ultimate personal glory. Daemons already possess the immortality that represents the pinnacle of a Warrior's Path. But for their part, daemons crave the freedom of the Warriors, because each daemon is shackled to the will of its superiors.

So while the two forces do often make natural allies, such alliances tend to fragment into jealous rivalries more often than they endure.

What proportion of Warriors are not human? Are other species drawn to specific gods?

No one has successfully completed a comprehensive survey of Warrior demographics, or even attempted one, but non-human Warriors are common enough in battle – the numbers vary greatly from region to region. All sapient species have the capacity to worship darkness and disorder, and possess souls that can be sworn in exchange for a Warrior's power.

There seems to be some basis to the generalisations of ogres being drawn to Gluttony, elves admiring the god of Pride and so forth. But these are rough guidelines at best – the truth is much more complex, as individuals of all species can find temptation in any of the seven sins.

RECENT CONFLICTS

Herr Sage, what are the most recent wars of the Ninth Age?

So you wish for tales of conflict and bloodshed? Alas, it seems all too common a request. There is war and fresh conflict somewhere in the world at almost all times – but a comprehensive catalogue would require a certain additional fee… Or perhaps you could purchase my highly anticipated tome on the subject, soon to be published by Leadgut and Son. For now, allow me to present a brief summary of the choicest and bloodiest affairs from recent years.

About ten years ago there was quite the hew and cry from the dwarves at Nevaz Vanez when they found their slopes covered in sapling trees. Attempts to uproot and plough their fields were emphatically prevented by hails of arrows and roving gangs of thicket beasts. The sylvan aggressors enjoyed the upper hand over several skirmishes, until the Hold engineers produced a number of quite devastating flame cannons. After defeating the elves in spectacular, if somewhat horrifying fashion, the engineers declared the "problem solved".

Mind you, I can still remember the occasion, several years before that, when it was the sylvans who prevailed in a substantial conflict. It involved a long series of battles against a major beast herd in southern Sonnstahl, each side using their powers of stealth to repeatedly ambush the other. Much of Narrenwald's forests were left in ruin, though they soon recovered after the elves butchered the last of the herd. I heard it all started because the beasts had foolishly tried to forage a grove sacred to the Trewi gods. Heisermann claims it was an intentional slight to provoke a battle, but then Heisermann does seem to specialise in being provoking.

That war was only one of the herds' depredations that finally resulted in the Emperor's decree in 953 to drive the beasts from the eastern bog where they've lurked for so long. The terrain had long been impenetrable, but on this occasion, the Imperial army found a beast guide willing to betray his own herd, and lead them through the marsh. It didn't help – the few wretched Sonnstahler survivors staggered back with tales of slaughter. But it's said that despite the mighty victory, no tales are told of the treacherous informant, whose name was never spoken by the beasts again: the ultimate dishonour in a culture built on stories.

Sonnstahl has found more success overseas. Jealous of Destria's new wealth, Matthias' father Emperor Frederick sent galleons to explore Virentia many years ago. Close to the Shattered Sea, they found local tribes growing "schokoatl" and other desirable crops. Trade negotiations were aborted after a covert inquisitor discovered that one of the natives revered Nukuja. The whole tribe was mercilessly hanged on his orders, except a dozen prisoners kept for their knowledge of the plants' cultivation. The tables turned with the appearance of a large band of Warriors from the north; whether in response or by coincidence is not clear. But the settlers were spared their comeuppance by the arrival of ships with fresh troops and gunpowder, and the Sonnstahlers were able to drive the warband off. Today their holdings have grown into the remarkably profitable colony of Fredericksberg.

Around the same time, I heard that an entirely separate Warrior army had been sighted in the Great Desert. Instead of attacking the wealthy empires to the north and south as usual, this army instead marched east and dared to pit itself against the undying forces of Naptesh. In this it

achieved a remarkable victory, even seizing Queen Mahatesh's ouroboros diadem from the Temple of Nephet-Ra in Djedesh. It's claimed that a certain champion ascended as an Exalted Herald at about this date, but the damnable – ahem, I mean judicious – Inquisition appears to have repressed any trustworthy reports on this point.

Only a few years later, the desert sands were disturbed again, when engineers from the Blasted Plain began a long-planned project to extend the Steel Road west into Taphria. The Infernals' scheme was cut short when it approached the lost cities of Naptesh, the dwarves and their slaves sharing the fate of all who disturb the slumber of the dead. Undaunted, they returned again with a large military expedition to safeguard the works. According to Luccini's goblin servant, the ensuing battle was truly dreadful, lasting many days, but eventually the Infernal army was overwhelmed, and nothing now remains of it but sun-bleached bones.

Many of the kadim used in this and other Infernal engagements were first bound several decades ago, when we received reports of daemonic battalions rampaging in the north of the Blasted Plain. The mystic explanation was that Savar himself had attempted to subdue the supernals loyal to the Vaneb gods, and the conflict in the Immortal Realm erupted through the very Inferno, across the Veil and into Infernal territory. Desperate for aid, a significant number of kadim agreed to the dwarves' terms of binding, and together they assembled a host that repelled the legions of Pride, banishing the daemon army back across the Veil and deep into the bowels of Hell.

But the forces of Darkness are never cowed for long, and a few years ago we heard they had emerged again from the Wasteland, this time engaging a large party of ogres that was searching the lost city of Hyiteng, the ancient capital of Qenghet Khan's legendary ogre empire. Unlike that famous conqueror, these ogres were savagely defeated by the united legions of the Seven, their deeds inspiring Dark believers around the world. Still, we hear that other expeditions have enjoyed more success in Hyiteng since then – even if the coxcombs in the

Exotic History Department continue to ignorantly deny such a place ever existed.

Also successful was an ogre assault on Dathen a little while back. Though the news is second-hand, we understand that the power of the ogres native to Silexia was augmented by tribes of visiting nomads from Augea (having crossed the icy polar regions by foot in one of their rare but mighty treks), until a great tide of flesh broke through the fortresses and border defenders of the dread elves and sacked the wealthy trading city of Balnarath, seizing its supplies and freeing its slaves. Many elves went hungry that winter, they say.

But it remains much more common for the Daeb to raid than to be raided. In one remarkable example, a Republic fleet harbouring in the Tanna archipelago, which stretches south of Khomnan and Tsuandan, heard legends of a hidden power from their human captives. Searching the island, their airbourne scouts discovered a secret saurian enclave; one particularly dextrous pegasus was able to learn the concealed entrance and escape the guards. Forcing their way into the reptiles' ancient stronghold with much bloodshed, the raiders successfully plundered the once-mighty site, taking many scaled slaves and expanding their menagerie with several cold-blooded gigantic curiosities. An eerie display of the long reach of Daeb power, no matter what the politicians may say.

It's yet to be determined whether saurians have a concept of revenge; their actions are always difficult to comprehend. Recently in Sagarika, the goblin Garden of Shamalmar suffered a stampede of magna sauria and its inhabitants were driven out, for no clear reason. The saurians let them go in peace; they preserved as many of the plants as possible, transporting them to another location to create a new Garden there. We can only surmise that the Garden's previous location did not fit in the saurians' unfathomable schemes! Of course, they failed to understand the suspicious minds of the goblins. Unable to trust a Garden

built by others, they rejected this sanctuary and instead chose to become hobgoblins in the service of Bashib Kegnat citadel. Luccini's goblin says his old mother still lives there, which is a curious turn of phrase, since Warborn cannot know their mothers.

Another goblin tale was heard from the Forsaken Marches, where both Warborn and Vermin hold great power. A clash was inevitable; goblins from the Garden of One Thousand Caves, together with a large allied orc tribe, descended upon the rodents and annihilated several cohorts from the Third-And-A-Half Legion, as well as the darkstone mines they defended. Both military and surveillance assets have been observed to reinforce the region since then, presumably sent by the Vermin Senate, and conflict may yet escalate again. But the mines have collapsed for good, and so new sources of darkstone are likely being explored elsewhere.

We hear that Avrasi standards have even been raised as far away as Silexia, after large numbers of vermin managed to escape Daeb slavery and flee west. After building a protective warren in a large mesa formation, the rats soon learned that the elves are far from the only threat in the land. Clashes with a human tribe nearby revealed the presence of a vampiric skin-walker affiliated with a new world Covenant chapter, who took animal forms and raised corpses to make war upon the mesa-fortress. The night creature was finally destroyed when the vermin erupted forth at dawn, if we believe the telling in recent admiralty dispatches.

The Covenant is also operating in Virentia, as reported by my contacts in Aldan. When Highborn trading concerns learned of discontent among local human suppliers of rare elastic materials from the rainforest, the Royal Marines were sent to secure their cooperation. But they found the frightened natives under attack from a blood-drinking jungle monster of bat-like form, and shuffling waves of the moaning dead. With each slain elf returning to attack its comrades, the marines made a valiant stand but were completely destroyed, with only a single sky sloop returning to tell the tale.

By contrast, when the Pearl Throne attacked Vetia at the behest of the Imperial faction, they remained as victors. I refer of course to the seizure of Calperon, an island off the coast of Brezanne, several decades ago. Considered a holy place by the Equitans, battle was joined at land and sea, but the elves' overwhelming naval superiority proved decisive. Today, it remains an important supply port for the Royal Navy, known as Racentash Reb, and the Highborn also claim to have restored ancient temples proving that the island is as spiritually important to the elves as it is to the followers of the Lady.

The Lady is not known to easily countenance defeat, of course. Her Equitan armies have won many glorious victories – perhaps more often as invader than defender, it must be said. I remember the story of one expedition hunting

Covenant agents in Destria, which accidentally offended the dwarven outpost of Kinaz Dun when it passed through the Crimson Peaks. On the return journey, the Equitan rearguard was met by a throng of Hold dwarves, assembled by a famous Seeker to right the wrong that had been committed. After a heroic stand, the humans were on the point of oblivion when the main force of their army arrived, flying colours said to have been mystically endowed by the legendary Roland, and it was the dwarves who found themselves crushed. Many knights earned their spurs that day, and the bards still go on about it at the Red Griffon most Venadi nights.

I hope this brief venture through the web of conflicts that shapes the world today has been enough to sate your bloodlust – whoops, I mean your curiosity, at least for the time being. Don't forget to enquire with Leadgut about more to come!

THE 9TH AGE
FANTASY BATTLES

ASK THE SAGE

Education is a fine thing, and the citizens of Avras are naturally curious. Many are the questions they have about the strange peoples and places we find today in the Ninth Age. To shine a light on such matters, we naturally turned to the legendary Sigmund "The Sage" Selig, that most good natured and fair-minded of scholars, who can be found in his rather cramped offices above the Unnatural Philosophy department on Via Urbana.

The Background Book Serie: **The Rulebook Serie:**

Please search by book Title
Please search by book Title

Please search by book Title

Si vous préférez lire en français, jetez un œil ici :

Sera disponible bientôt.

Si prefieres leer en español, échale un vistazo aquí:

Falls du lieber in Deutsch liest, schaue doch am besten hier:

Compatible with
IX
AGE
TM
The 9th Age TM

www.ingramcontent.com/pod-product-compliance
Lightning Source LLC
LaVergne TN
LVHW080613200726
843509LV00007B/298